P9-BZI-730

E   Crummel,
CRU   Susan Stevens.
           City dog,
           country dog

Middletown Library
Service Center
786 South Main Street
Middletown, CT 06457

City Dog, Country Dog

Adapted from an Aesop Fable

Story by **Susan Stevens Crummel**
and **Dorothy Donohue**

Illustrations by **Dorothy Donohue**

Middletown Library
Service Center
786 South Main Street
Middletown, CT 06457

Marshall Cavendish

New York . . . London . . . Singapore

**For Cecilee, French teacher extraordinaire and loyal friend through the years. Merci!
Special thanks to Dorothy for her inspiration, talent, and affability!**
— S.S.C.

To Sandy for her enthusiastic support, and thanks to Albert Lee for his generosity
— D.D.

Text copyright © 2004 by Susan Stevens Crummel
Illustrations copyright © 2004 by Dorothy Donohue
All rights reserved.
Marshall Cavendish
99 White Plains Road
Tarrytown, New York 10591
www.marshallcavendish.com

Thanks to The Bridgeman Art Library International and Art Resource, NY, for granting permission to reproduce the following paintings on the final page of this book: "The Starry Night" (Digital Image © The Museum of Modern Art / Licensed by SCALA / Art Resource, NY); "Vase with Irises" (Art Resource, NY); "Sunflowers" (Scala / Art Resource, NY); "Jane Avril at the Jardin de Paris" (Private Collection / The Stapleton Collection / Bridgeman Art Library); "Actress Marcelle Lander" (Scala / Art Resource, NY); "Portrait of Vincent van Gogh" (Stedelijk Museum, Amsterdam, The Netherlands / Interfoto / Bridgeman Art Library).

Library of Congress Cataloging-in-Publication Data

Crummel, Susan Stevens.
City dog, country dog / written by Susan Stevens Crummel ; illustrated by Dorothy Donohue.
p. cm.
Summary: Two French dogs, Henri and Vincent, meet at art school and become good friends despite their differences.
ISBN 0-7614-5156-0
[1. Dogs—Fiction. 2. Friendship—Fiction. 3. Artists—Fiction.] I.Donohue, Dorothy, ill. II. Title.
PZ7.C88845To 2004
[E]—dc22   2003011631

The text in this book is set in Invoice.
The art is created with textured papers, layered and pasted down.
The paintings are rendered in acrylic paint and colored pencils.

Book design by Virginia Pope

Printed in China
First edition
2 4 6 5 3 1

Remember me? I'm Country Mouse. You know, the star of *Town Mouse, Country Mouse*? I'll let you in on a little secret. That tale was really about two dogs! Two very different dogs who had one thing in common— they loved to paint. At least that's what this fellow named Aesop told me.

It all began long ago, in the country of France . . .

It was the first day of art school.
Henri T. LaPooch was from the city.
Vincent van Dog was from the country.
"Bonjour!" barked Madame Fifi,
the art teacher.

"BONE? Did she say BONE?"
woofed Vincent. "YUM!"

"What a bonehead!" Henri
yapped under his breath.

"Écoutez!" barked Madame
Fifi. "You're making too much
noise! Go clean the paintbrushes.
You two are in the doghouse!"

And that's how the two artists
became friends. Very different
friends.

Bonjour (bohn-ZHOOR) means Good day
Écoutez! (ay-koo-TAY) means Listen!

Vincent was tall.
Henri was short.

Vincent used fat,
thick globs of paint.
Henri used tiny,
thin lines of paint.

Vincent liked quiet.
Henri liked noise.

Vincent painted
beautiful flowers.
Henri painted
beautiful dancers.

But they didn't mind being different.
"C'est la vie!" they howled.
On the last day of school,
they made sketches of each other.
"Au revoir," whimpered
Henri. "I'll miss you."
"I promise to write!"
Vincent woofed.

And he kept his promise.

C'est la vie! (seh lah VEE) means That's life!
Au revoir (oh VWAHR) means Good-bye

June 8

Dear Vincent,

I would love to come to
the country! By the way,
what is a picnic?

Your friend,
Henri

P.S. I'll wear my
special black tie.

To: Vincent van Dog
1 Lazy Lane
The Country

The two friends were so glad to see
each other that they wagged their tails
and rolled on the ground!

"You must be hungry." Vincent grabbed Henri's paw. "Come on—the picnic is ready!"

He brought baskets and baskets of fresh vegetables from the garden.

Henri pointed to a basket, "Excusez-moi, what is this green stuff?"

"Why, spinach and brussels sprouts—my favorites. Here, have a BIG helping!"

"POUAH!" Henri yapped. "But where are the forks?"

"Forks? Who needs forks? I just woof it down!"

Henri howled, "THERE ARE ANTS ON MY FOOD!"

"Eat 'em." Vincent licked his chops. "They make it crunchy!"

"I'm feeling sick as a dog," moaned Henri.

Excusez-moi (ex-cue-zay MWAH) means Excuse me

Pouah! (PWAH) means Yuck!

"You look tired as a dog, too," barked Vincent. "Come on, I'll show you my favorite place to nap!"

"Excusez-moi," Henri yapped. "Where's the bed? "

"The ground," woofed Vincent.

"May I have a pillow, s'il vous plaît?"

"Pillow? Who needs a pillow? Just lean against the haystack like this!"

"Ah-ah-ah-cho-o-o-o!

I'm not tired anymore," whined Henri.

S'il vous plaît (seel voo PLEY) means Please

"It's getting dark— let's have some fun!" Vincent scampered up a hill.

"Where's the excitement?" Henri panted, looking around.

"Look at the starry night," sighed Vincent.

"It's too quiet!" Henri yapped.

"Shh-shh-shh!"

"This isn't fun," whimpered Henri. "I'm going back to the city! Bonsoir."

Bonsoir (bohn-SWAHR) means Good night

June 21

Dear Vincent,
I'm sorry I left so quickly!
The country is not for me.
Why don't you come to the
city? We'll put on the dog and
paint the town red!

Your friend,
Henri

TO: Vincent van Dog
1 Lazy Lane
The Country

June 28

Dear Henri,

That sounds fun! I'll
bring all my red paint.
Your buddy,
Vincent

To: Henri T. LaPooch
qqq Party Place
The City

The two friends were so glad to see each other that they wagged their tails, rolled on the ground, and jumped in the air!

"You must be hungry." Henri grabbed Vincent's paw. "Come on, let's go to my favorite restaurant—Café Bow-Wow!"

The waiter brought trays and trays of rich food.

Vincent pointed to a tray. "What are those squishy brown things?"

"Escargots. They are très bons!"

Vincent pointed again. "What's this?"

"A mousse."

"A moose?" barked Vincent. "Where are the horns?"

"Try the fondue," yapped Henri.

"I'm not fond of fondue," whined Vincent. "My tummy hurts."

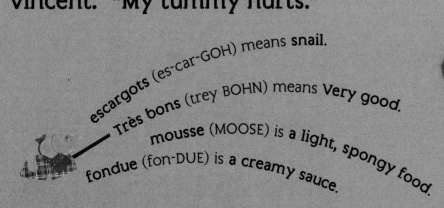

escargots (es-car-GOH) means snail.

Très bons (trey BOHN) means very good.

mousse (MOOSE) is a light, spongy food.

fondue (fon-DUE) is a creamy sauce.

"I know just the cure!"
Henri bounded out the
door and down the street.
"My favorite spot, the
Moulin Rouge!"
   "Wow!" barked
Vincent. "What's
all that noise?"
   "It's a party!"
Henri yelped.
"Let's go inside.
Tout de suite!" Henri
dragged Vincent inside.

Moulin Rouge (moo-lahn ROUGE) means Red Mill
Tout de suite (toot dih SWEET) means Right away

"Bring on the can-can cats!" howled Henri.

Out came a line of dancers kicking and turning. The crowd went wild. Everyone began to clap and sway with the music. "Let's dance!" Henri pulled Vincent onto the stage.

"Zut alors!" growled the owner. "You mutts get off that stage or I'll throw you out!"

But Henri didn't hear— he was having too much fun. And Vincent didn't hear— it was way too noisy.

Zut alors! (zut a-LOHR) means MY goodness!

The owner grabbed the two dogs and booted them out into the street.

"Ouch!" yelped Vincent as he landed on his ear. "Stars—I'm seeing stars! Am I home? Oh, no—I'm still in the city."

"Oui," Henri replied.

"We?" Vincent whimpered. "There's no more WE! I'm going back to the country! Bonjour, bonsoir, au revoir— Good day, good night, GOOD BYE!"

Oui (WEE) means Yes

The two friends were so glad to see
each other that they wagged their tails,
rolled on the ground, jumped in the air,
and howled at the top of their lungs!

"To us," woofed Vincent.

"Oui," Henri yapped. "Best friends forever!"

Well, that about wraps it up.

Oh, I almost forgot! Every fable has a moral—you know, a lesson to be learned. Hm-m-m-m. How about . . .

You can't teach an old dog new tricks? No, that's not it.

It's a dog-eat-dog world? Ooh, that's kind of scary.

Every dog has its day? Not quite.

I've got it!

Vive la différence! (veev lah dee-fay-RONCE) That means Hooray for differences!

Jane Avril at the Jardin de Paris
by Henri de Toulouse-Lautrec

Actress Marcelle Lander
by Henri de Toulouse-Lautrec

Portrait of Vincent van Gogh
by Henri de Toulouse-Lautrec

Vincent van Dog and Henri T. LaPooch are based on two real-life artists named **Vincent van Gogh** (GO) and **Henri de Toulouse-Lautrec** (too-LOOSE-loh-TREK). Although Vincent was born in the Netherlands, he moved to Paris, where he became friends with Henri in 1886. They attended the same studio and studied Impressionism—a type of modern art made with quick brush strokes to give an impression of a scene rather than an exact copy of it. Vincent and Henri were among a group of artists known as Post-impressionists. Henri painted his posterlike paintings, such as "Jane Avril at the Jardin de Paris," with thin lines and flat colors. Vincent, on the other hand, favored thick, swirling paint strokes and bold colors, such as those found in "The Starry Night."

Vincent grew tired of Paris and moved to Provence in 1888. The two artists wrote letters back and forth. They remained friends until Vincent's death in 1890, at the age of thirty-seven. Henri died eleven years later in 1901, two months shy of his thirty-seventh birthday.

Henri T. LaPooch's and Vincent van Dog's paintings are similar to those painted by Henri de Toulouse-Lautrec and Vincent van Gogh. Look though the pages of this book and see if you can find the dogs' versions of the six famous paintings shown on this page. Can you find others?

The Starry Night
by Vincent van Gogh

Vase with Irises
by Vincent van Gogh

Sunflowers
by Vincent van Gogh